Shoemaker Martin

Based on a story by Leo Tolstoy
Illustrated by
Bernadette Watts

North-South Books

Shoemaker Martin

Based on a story by Leo Tolstoy

Adapted by Brigitte Hanhart
Translated by Michael Hale

Illustrated by
Bernadette Watts

North-South Books
New York   London   Toronto   Melbourne

In a small town in Russia there once lived a man named Martin, who earned his living mending shoes. He lived and worked in a basement room. Through the window, all he could see of the people passing by were their legs. But he still recognized most of them, as there was scarcely a pair of boots or shoes in town that he had not mended at one time or another.

Martin worked all day until it became too dark for him to see his work. Then he would make a pot of tea, light the lamp and take down his big Bible from the shelf. He read many pages, and the more he read, the happier he felt.

One winter evening he went on reading till it was very late, and he reached the story of the rich man who invited Jesus into his home. Martin thought hard.

"If Jesus came to visit me, what would I say? What would I do? How would I welcome him?"

Still thinking about this, Martin fell asleep.

"Martin!" called a voice suddenly. Martin woke up. But no one was there. Then he heard the voice again. It said, "Make sure you watch the street tomorrow, because I shall be coming!"

Martin sat up and rubbed his eyes. Had he really heard those words or was it just a dream? He looked carefully round the room but saw nobody. He turned out the lamp and soon went back to sleep.

The next morning Martin got up very early, before dawn. He lit the stove and put the kettle of water on it. As he ate his breakfast he looked out of the window, wondering whether it had been a dream last night, or whether he really would see some unfamiliar shoes belonging to a very special stranger.

Still pondering, he set to work. Just as he was cutting a piece of leather, Martin heard footsteps outside. He looked up, but saw only poor old Stefan the street sweeper. Stefan was stamping his feet and blowing into his freezing hands in an effort to get warm.

Quickly, Martin opened the window and called, "Come on in, Stefan, and warm up a bit. The kettle's just boiling!"

Stefan staggered in.

"Don't bother to wipe your feet. Sit down by the stove!"

Stefan sipped the hot tea that Martin gave him, and when he felt warm again, he thanked Martin gratefully before leaving.

"Don't mention it! Come any time," replied Martin.

Martin drank a cup of tea himself, then made some cabbage soup for later. When next he looked out of the window, he saw a young woman standing huddled out in the bad weather with a baby in her arms. She was trying to wrap the baby up to shelter it from the cold wind, but she scarcely had anything to wrap it in except her thin, shabby dress.

Martin went up to the door and called her in.

He gave her some of his hot soup and brought his old coat to put round her shoulders. It was big enough to protect her and the baby. Afterwards he played with the baby and made it laugh. Finally Martin fetched some money from an old trunk and gave it to the mother to buy milk.

The poor woman bowed and thanked Martin most gratefully before she left, feeling much better.

Martin finished off the soup and cleared away the dishes. Later, as he sat at work again, a shadow fell across the window, and Martin looked up eagerly, but it was just townsfolk passing. Some of them he knew, and some he didn't, but nobody in particular caught his attention or seemed like a special visitor.

All at once he heard shouting outside on the street. A market woman was dragging along a poorly dressed boy who had stolen one of her apples. She tugged him by his hair, and the boy protested and struggled to get away.

Martin hurried out and separated them. "Let him go, grand-mother," he begged. "He won't do it again. If we punish someone so harshly for taking an apple, what punishments should we expect for our sins that are far, far worse?"

The boy and the woman looked at Martin and then looked at each other. Quietly, the boy asked the old woman to forgive him and offered to carry her basket along the road.

Martin wanted to finish stitching one of the boots which had to be delivered tomorrow. Soon it was dark. The lamplighter passed by, lighting the streetlamps. Martin finished the boot. Then he put his tools away and swept the scraps of leather from the floor. He took down his lamp from the nail on the wall and placed it on the table so he could read once again the passage from the Bible which had been so much on his mind since last night.

Suddenly, he had the feeling that somebody was moving behind him. He looked round, and this time it really seemed there were some people in the room, but Martin could not make out who they were.

Then a voice whispered in his ear, "Martin, didn't you recognize me?"

"Whom?"

"Me!" And out of the shadows stepped Stefan, smiling.

"This was me too," the voice said again. And the woman with the baby came forward! She smiled and the baby laughed.

"And this was me as well," the voice said. And the old woman appeared together with the boy who had taken the apple. Both of them were smiling! Martin looked at them all in amazement, and then each one vanished.

Then the shoemaker realized that his dream had come true after all. Jesus really had visited him that day, and he, Martin, had taken him in. Martin was overcome with joy.

He began reading from the Bible where it had fallen open. It was a different page from the one he had read last night. At the top of the page he read: "Inasmuch as ye have done it unto the least of these my brethren, ye have done it unto me."

End

First published in the United States, Great Britain, Canada, Australia and New Zealand in 1986 by North-South Books, an imprint of Rada Matija AG.
Reprinted in 1987.

Distributed in the United States by
Henry Holt and Company, Inc., 521 Fifth Avenue,
New York, New York 10175.
Library of Congress Catalog Card Number: 86-60489.

ISBN 0-8050-0040-2

Distributed in Great Britain by
Blackie and Son Ltd, 7 Leicester Place,
London WC 2H 7BP.
British Library Cataloguing in Publication Data

Hanhart, Brigitte
  Shoemaker Martin.
  I. Title   II. Watts, Bernadette
  III. Hale, Michael   IV. Tolstoy, L. N.
  833'.914 [J]   PZ7

ISBN 0-200-72892-X

Distributed in Canada by
Douglas & McIntyre Ltd., Toronto.
Canadian Cataloguing in Publication Data available in
Marc Record from National Library of Canada.
ISBN 0 88894 774 7

Distributed in Australia and New Zealand by
Buttercup Books Pty. Ltd., Melbourne.
ISBN 0 949447 28 5

Copyright © 1986 Nord-Süd Verlag, Mönchaltorf, Switzerland
First published in Switzerland under the title Schuster Martin
English text copyright © 1986 Michael Hale
Copyright English language edition under the imprint
North-South Books © 1986 Rada Matija AG, Staefa, Switzerland

Printed in Germany